AF363042

Ivan Alekseevich Bunin

The Gentleman from San Francisco, and Other Stories

e-artnow 2024

Ivan Alekseevich Bunin

The Gentleman from San Francisco, and Other Stories

e-artnow, 2024
Contact: eartnow.info@gmail.com

ISBN: 978-80-273-8820-2

Contents

GENTLE BREATHING 23

KASIMIR STANISLAVOVITCH 26

SON 31

"Woe to thee, Babylon, that mighty city!"

Apocalypse.

The gentleman from San Francisco--nobody either in Capri or Naples ever remembered his name--was setting out with his wife and daughter for the Old World, to spend there two years of pleasure.

He was fully convinced of his right to rest, to enjoy long and comfortable travels, and so forth. Because, in the first place he was rich, and in the second place, notwithstanding his fifty-eight years, he was just starting to live. Up to the present he had not lived, but only existed; quite well, it is true, yet with all his hopes on the future. He had worked incessantly--and the Chinamen whom he employed by the thousand in his factories knew what that meant. Now at last he realized that a great deal had been accomplished, and that he had almost reached the level of those whom he had taken as his ideals, so he made up his mind to pause for a breathing space. Men of his class usually began their enjoyments with a trip to Europe, India, Egypt. He decided to do the same. He wished naturally to reward himself in the first place for all his years of toil, but he was quite glad that his wife and daughter should also share in his pleasures. True, his wife was not distinguished by any marked susceptibilities, but then elderly American women are all passionate travellers. As for his daughter, a girl no longer young and somewhat delicate, travel was really necessary for her: apart from the question of health, do not happy meetings often take place in the course of travel? One may find one's self sitting next to a multimillionaire at table, or examining frescoes side by side with him.

The itinerary planned by the Gentleman of San Francisco was extensive. In December and January he hoped to enjoy the sun of southern Italy, the monuments of antiquity, the tarantella, the serenades of vagrant minstrels, and, finally, that which men of his age are most susceptible to, the love of quite young Neapolitan girls, even when the love is not altogether disinterestedly given. Carnival he thought of spending in Nice, in Monte Carlo, where at that season gathers the most select society, the precise society on which depend all the blessings of civilization--the fashion in evening dress, the stability of thrones, the declaration of wars, the prosperity of hotels; where some devote themselves passionately to automobile and boat races, others to roulette, others to what is called flirtation, and others to the shooting of pigeons which beautifully soar from their traps over emerald lawns, against a background of forget-me-not sea, instantly to fall, hitting the ground in little white heaps. The beginning of March he wished to devote to Florence, Passion Week in Rome, to hear the music of the Miserere; his plans also included Venice, Paris, bull-fights in Seville, bathing in the British Isles; then Athens, Constantinople, Egypt, even Japan ...certainly on his way home... . And everything at the outset went splendidly.

It was the end of November. Practically all the way to Gibraltar the voyage passed in icy darkness, varied by storms of wet snow. Yet the ship travelled well, even without much rolling. The passengers on board were many, and all people of some importance. The boat, the famous *Atlantis*, resembled a most expensive European hotel with all modern equipments: a night refreshment bar, Turkish baths, a newspaper printed on board; so that the days aboard the liner passed in the most select manner. The passengers rose early, to the sound of bugles sounding shrilly through the corridors in that grey twilit hour, when day was breaking slowly and sullenly over the grey-green, watery desert, which rolled heavily in the fog. Clad in their flannel pyjamas, the gentlemen took coffee, chocolate, or cocoa, then seated themselves in marble baths, did exercises, thereby whetting their appetite and their sense of well-being, made their toilet for the day, and proceeded to breakfast. Till eleven o'clock they were supposed to stroll cheerfully on deck, breathing the cold freshness of the ocean; or they played table-tennis or other games, that they might have an appetite for their eleven o'clock refreshment of sandwiches and bouillon; after which they read their newspaper with pleasure, and calmly awaited luncheon--which was a still more varied and nourishing meal than breakfast. The two hours which followed luncheon were devoted to rest. All the decks were crowded with lounge chairs on which lay passengers wrapped in plaids, looking at the mist-heavy sky or the foamy hillocks which flashed behind the bows, and dozing sweetly. Till five o'clock, when, refreshed and lively, they were treated to strong, fragrant tea and sweet cakes. At seven bugle-calls announced a dinner of nine courses. And now the Gentleman from San Francisco, rubbing his hands in a rising flush of vital forces, hastened to his state cabin to dress.

In the evening, the tiers of the *Atlantis* yawned in the darkness as with innumerable fiery eyes, and a multitude of servants in the kitchens, sculleries, wine-cellars, worked with a special frenzy. The ocean heaving beyond was terrible, but no one thought of it, firmly believing in the captain's power over it. The captain was a ginger-haired man of monstrous size and weight, apparently always torpid, who looked in his uniform with broad gold stripes very like a huge idol, and who rarely emerged from his mysterious chambers to show himself to the passengers. Every minute the siren howled from the bows with hellish moroseness, and screamed with fury, but few diners heard it--it was drowned by the sounds of an excellent string band, exquisitely and untiringly playing in the huge two-tiered hall that was decorated with marble and covered with velvet carpets, flooded with feasts of light from crystal chandeliers and gilded girandoles, and crowded with ladies in bare shoulders and jewels, with men in dinner-jackets, elegant waiters and respectful *maîtres d'hôtel*, one of whom, he who took the wine-orders only, wore a chain round his neck like a lord mayor. Dinner-jacket and perfect linen made the Gentleman from San Francisco look much younger. Dry, of small stature, badly built but strongly made, polished to a glow and in due measure animated, he sat in the golden-pearly radiance of this palace, with a bottle of amber Johannisberg at his hand, and glasses, large and small, of delicate crystal, and a curly bunch of fresh hyacinths. There was something Mongolian in his yellowish face with its trimmed silvery moustache, large teeth blazing with gold, and strong bald head blazing like old ivory. Richly dressed, but in keeping with her age, sat his wife, a big, broad, quiet woman. Intricately, but lightly and transparently dressed, with an innocent immodesty, sat his daughter, tall, slim, her magnificent hair splendidly done, her breath fragrant with violet cachous, and the tenderest little rosy moles showing near her lip and between her bare, slightly powdered shoulder blades. The dinner lasted two whole hours, to be followed by dancing in the ball-room, whence the men, including, of course, the Gentleman from San Francisco, proceeded to the bar; there, with their feet cocked up on the tables, they settled the destinies of nations in the course of their political and stock-exchange conversations, smoking meanwhile Havana cigars and drinking liqueurs till they were crimson in the face, waited on all the while by negroes in red jackets with eyes like peeled, hard-boiled eggs. Outside, the ocean heaved in black mountains; the snow-storm hissed furiously in the clogged cordage; the steamer trembled in every fibre as she surmounted these watery hills and struggled with the storm, ploughing through the moving masses which every now and then reared in front of her, foam-crested. The siren, choked by the fog, groaned in mortal anguish. The watchmen in the look-out towers froze with cold, and went mad with their super-human straining of attention. As the gloomy and sultry depths of the inferno, as the ninth circle, was the submerged womb of the steamer, where gigantic furnaces roared and dully giggled, devouring with their red-hot maws mountains of coal cast hoarsely in by men naked to the waist, bathed in their own corrosive dirty sweat, and lurid with the purple-red reflection of flame. But in the refreshment bar men jauntily put their feet up on the tables, showing their patent-leather pumps, and sipped cognac or other liqueurs, and swam in waves of fragrant smoke as they chatted in well-bred manner. In the dancing hall light and warmth and joy were poured over everything; couples turned in the waltz or writhed in the tango, while the music insistently, shamelessly, delightfully, with sadness entreated for one, only one thing, one and the same thing all the time. Amongst this resplendent crowd was an ambassador, a little dry modest old man; a great millionaire, clean-shaven, tall, of an indefinite age, looking like a prelate in his old-fashioned dress-coat; also a famous Spanish author, and an international beauty already the least bit faded, of unenviable reputation; finally an exquisite loving couple, whom everybody watched curiously because of their unconcealed happiness: *he* danced only with *her*, and sang, with great skill, only to *her* accompaniment, and everything about them seemed so charming!–and only the captain knew that this couple had been engaged by the steamship company to play at love for a good salary, and that they had been sailing for a long time, now on one liner, now on another.

At Gibraltar the sun gladdened them all: it was like early spring. A new passenger appeared on board, arousing general interest. He was a hereditary prince of a certain Asiatic state, travelling incognito: a small man, as if all made of wood, though his movements were alert; broad-faced, in gold-rimmed glasses, a little unpleasant because of his large black moustache which was sparse and transparent like that of a corpse; but on the whole inoffensive, simple, modest. In the Mediterranean they met once more the breath of winter. Waves, large and florid as the tail of a peacock, waves with snow-white crests heaved under the impulse of the tramontane wind, and came merrily, madly rushing towards the ship, in the bright lustre of a perfectly clear sky. The next day the sky began to pale, the horizon grew dim, land was approaching: Ischia, Capri could be seen through the glasses, then Naples herself, looking like pieces of sugar strewn at the foot of some dove-coloured mass; whilst beyond, vague and deadly white with snow, a range of distant mountains. The decks were crowded. Many ladies and gentlemen were putting on light fur-trimmed coats. Noiseless Chinese servant boys, bandy-legged, with pitch-black plaits hanging down to their heels, and with girlish thick eyebrows, unobtrusively came and went, carrying up the stairways plaids, canes, valises, hand-bags of crocodile leather, and never speaking above a whisper. The daughter of the Gentleman from San Francisco stood side by side with the prince, who, by a happy circumstance, had been introduced to her the previous evening. She had the air of one looking fixedly into the distance towards something which he was pointing out to her, and which he was explaining hurriedly, in a low voice. Owing to his size, he looked amongst the rest like a boy. Altogether he was not handsome, rather queer, with his spectacles, bowler hat, and English coat, and then the hair of his sparse moustache just like horse-hair, and the swarthy, thin skin of his face seeming stretched over his features and slightly varnished. But the girl listened to him, and was so excited that she did not know what he was saying. Her heart beat with incomprehensible rapture because of him, because he was standing next to her and talking to her, to her alone. Everything, everything about him was so unusual--his dry hands, his clean skin under which flowed ancient, royal blood, even his plain, but somehow particularly tidy European dress; everything was invested with an indefinable glamour, with all that was calculated to enthrall a young woman. The Gentleman from San Francisco, wearing for his part a silk hat and grey spats over patent-leather shoes, kept eyeing the famous beauty who stood near him, a tall, wonderful figure, blonde, with her eyes painted according to the latest Parisian fashion, holding on a silver chain a tiny, cringing, hairless little dog, to which she was addressing herself all the time. And the daughter, feeling some vague embarrassment, tried not to notice her father.

Like all Americans, he was very liberal with his money when travelling. And like all of them, he believed in the full sincerity and good-will of those who brought his food and drinks, served him from morn till night, anticipated his smallest desire, watched over his cleanliness and rest, carried his things, called the porters, conveyed his trunks to the hotels. So it was everywhere, so it was during the voyage, so it ought to be in Naples. Naples grew and drew nearer. The brass band, shining with the brass of their instruments, had already assembled on deck. Suddenly they deafened everybody with the strains of their triumphant rag-time. The giant captain appeared in full uniform on the bridge, and like a benign pagan idol waved his hands to the passengers in a gesture of welcome. And to the Gentleman from San Francisco, as well as to every other passenger, it seemed as if for him alone was thundered forth that rag-time march, so greatly beloved by proud America; for him alone the Captain's hand waved, welcoming him on his safe arrival. Then, when at last the *Atlantis* entered port and veered her many-tiered mass against the quay that was crowded with expectant people, when the gangways began their rattling--ah, then what a lot of porters and their assistants in caps with golden galloons, what a lot of all sorts of commissionaires, whistling boys, and sturdy ragamuffins with packs of postcards in their hands rushed to meet the Gentleman from San Francisco with offers of their services! With what amiable contempt he grinned at those ragamuffins as he walked to the automobile of the very same hotel at which the prince would probably put up, and calmly muttered between his teeth, now in English, now in Italian--"Go away! Via!"

Life at Naples started immediately in the set routine. Early in the morning, breakfast in a gloomy dining-room with a draughty damp wind blowing in from the windows that opened on to a little stony garden: a cloudy, unpromising day, and a crowd of guides at the doors of the vestibule. Then the first smiles of a warm, pinky-coloured sun, and from the high, overhanging balcony a view of Vesuvius, bathed to the feet in the radiant vapours of the morning sky, while beyond, over the silvery-pearly ripple of the bay, the subtle outline of Capri upon the horizon! Then nearer, tiny donkeys running in two-wheeled buggies away below on the sticky embankment, and detachments of tiny soldiers marching off with cheerful and defiant music.

After this a walk to the taxi-stand, and a slow drive along crowded, narrow, damp corridors of streets, between high, many-windowed houses. Visits to deadly-clean museums, smoothly and pleasantly lighted, but monotonously, as if from the reflection of snow. Or visits to churches, cold, smelling of wax, and always the same thing: a majestic portal, curtained with a heavy leather curtain: inside, a huge emptiness, silence, lonely little flames of clustered candles rud-dying the depths of the interior on some altar decorated with ribbon: a forlorn old woman amid dark benches, slippery gravestones under one's feet, and somebody's infallibly famous "Descent from the Cross." Luncheon at one o'clock on San Martino, where quite a number of the very selectest people gather about midday, and where once the daughter of the Gentleman from San Francisco almost became ill with joy, fancying she saw the prince sitting in the hall, although she knew from the newspapers that he had gone to Rome for a time. At five o'clock, tea in the hotel, in the smart salon where it was so warm, with the deep carpets and blazing fires. After which the thought of dinner--and again the powerful commanding voice of the gong heard over all the floors, and again strings of bare-shouldered ladies rustling with their silks on the staircases and reflecting themselves in the mirrors, again the wide-flung, hospitable, palatial dining-room, the red jackets of musicians on the platform, the black flock of waiters around the *maître d'hôtel*, who with extraordinary skill was pouring out a thick, roseate soup into soup-plates. The dinners, as usual, were the crowning event of the day. Every one dressed as if for a wedding, and so abundant were the dishes, the wines, the table-waters, sweetmeats, and fruit, that at about eleven o'clock in the evening the chamber-maids would take to every room rubber hot-water bottles, to warm the stomachs of those who had dined.

None the less, December of that year was not a success for Naples. The porters and sec-retaries were abashed if spoken to about the weather, only guiltily lifting their shoulders and murmuring that they could not possibly remember such a season; although this was not the first year they had had to make such murmurs, or to hint that "everywhere something terrible is happening." ...Unprecedented rains and storms on the Riviera, snow in Athens, Etna also piled with snow and glowing red at night; tourists fleeing from the cold of Palermo....The morning sun daily deceived the Neapolitans. The sky invariably grew grey towards midday, and fine rain began to fall, falling thicker and colder. The palms of the hotel approach glistened like wet tin; the city seemed peculiarly dirty and narrow, the museums excessively dull; the cigar-ends of the fat cab-men, whose rubber rain-capes flapped like wings in the wind, seemed insufferably stinking, the energetic cracking of whips over the ears of thin-necked horses sounded altogether false, and the clack of the shoes of the signorini who cleaned the tram-lines quite horrible, while the women, walking through the mud, with their black heads uncovered in the rain, seemed disgustingly short-legged: not to mention the stench and dampness of foul fish which drifted from the quay where the sea was foaming. The gentleman and lady from San Francisco began to bicker in the mornings; their daughter went about pale and head-achey, and then roused up again, went into raptures over everything, and was lovely, charming. Charming were those tender, complicated feelings which had been aroused in her by the meeting with the plain little man in whose veins ran such special blood. But after all, does it matter *what* awakens a maiden soul--whether it is money, fame, or noble birth?...Everybody declared that in Sorrento, or in Capri, it was quite different. There it was warmer, sunnier, the lemon-trees were in bloom, the morals were purer, the wine unadulterated. So behold, the family from San Francisco decided to go with all their trunks to Capri, after which they would return and settle down in Sorrento: when they had seen Capri, trodden the stones where stood Tiberius' palaces, visited the famous caves of the Blue Grotto, and listened to the pipers from Abruzzi, who wander about the isle during the month of the Nativity, singing the praises of the Virgin.

On the day of departure--a very memorable day for the family from San Francisco--the sun did not come out even in the morning. A heavy fog hid Vesuvius to the base, and came greying low over the leaden heave of the sea, whose waters were concealed from the eye at a distance of half a mile. Capri was completely invisible, as if it had never existed on earth. The little steamer that was making for the island tossed so violently from side to side that the family from San Francisco lay like stones on the sofas in the miserable saloon of the tiny boat, their feet wrapped in plaids, and their eyes closed. The lady, as she thought, suffered worst of all, and several times was overcome with sickness. It seemed to her that she was dying. But the stewardess who came to and fro with the basin, the stewardess who had been for years, day in, day out, through heat and cold, tossing on these waves, and who was still indefatigable, even kind to every one--she only smiled. The younger lady from San Francisco was deathly pale, and held in her teeth a slice of lemon. Now not even the thought of meeting the prince at Sorrento, where he was due to arrive by Christmas, could gladden her. The gentleman lay flat on his back, in a broad overcoat and a flat cap, and did not loosen his jaws throughout the voyage. His face grew dark, his moustache white, his head ached furiously. For the last few days, owing to the bad weather, he had been drinking heavily, and had more than once admired the "tableaux vivants." The rain whipped on the rattling window-panes, under which water dripped on to the sofas, the wind beat the masts with a howl, and at moments, aided by an onrushing wave, laid the little steamer right on its side, whereupon something would roll noisily away below. At the stopping places, Castellamare, Sorrento, things were a little better. But even the ship heaved frightfully, and the coast with all its precipices, gardens, pines, pink and white hotels, and hazy, curly green mountains swooped past the window, up and down, as it were on swings. The boats bumped against the side of the ship, the sailors and passengers shouted lustily, and somewhere a child, as if crushed to death, choked itself with screaming. The damp wind blew through the doors, and outside on the sea, from a reeling boat which showed the flag of the Hotel Royal, a fellow with guttural French exaggeration yelled unceasingly: "Rrroy-al! Hotel Rrroy-al!" intending to lure passengers aboard his craft. Then the Gentleman from San Francisco, feeling, as he ought to have felt, quite an old man, thought with anguish and spite of all these "Royals," "Splendids," "Excelsiors," and of these greedy, good-for-nothing, garlic-stinking fellows called Italians. Once, during a halt, on opening his eyes and rising from the sofa he saw under the rocky cliff-curtain of the coast a heap of such miserable stone hovels, all musty and mouldy, stuck on top of one another by the very water, among the boats, and the rags of all sorts, tin cans and brown fishing-nets, and, remembering that this was the very Italy he had come to enjoy, he was seized with despair....At last, in the twilight, the black mass of the island began to loom nearer, looking as if it were bored through at the base with little red lights. The wind grew softer, warmer, more sweet-smelling. Over the tamed waves, undulating like black oil, there came flowing golden boa-constrictors of light from the lanterns of the harbour....Then suddenly the anchor rumbled and fell with a splash into the water. Furious cries of the boatmen shouting against one another came from all directions. And relief was felt at once. The electric light of the cabin shone brighter, and a desire to eat, drink, smoke, move once more made itself felt....Ten minutes later the family from San Francisco disembarked into a large boat; in a quarter of an hour they had stepped on to the stones of the quay, and were soon seated in the bright little car of the funicular railway. With a buzz they were ascending the slope, past the stakes of the vineyards and wet, sturdy orange-trees, here and there protected by straw screens, past the thick glossy foliage and the brilliancy of orange fruits....Sweetly smells the earth in Italy after rain, and each of her islands has its own peculiar aroma.

The island of Capri was damp and dark that evening. For the moment, however, it had revived, and was lighted up here and there as usual at the hour of the steamer's arrival. At the top of the ascent, on the little piazza by the funicular station stood the crowd of those whose duty it was to receive with propriety the luggage of the Gentleman from San Francisco. There were other arrivals too, but none worthy of notice: a few Russians who had settled in Capri, untidy and absent-minded owing to their bookish thoughts, spectacled, bearded, half-buried in the upturned collars of their thick woollen overcoats. Then a group of long-legged, long-necked, round-headed German youths in Tirolese costumes, with knapsacks over their shoulders, needing no assistance, feeling everywhere at home and always economical in tips. The Gentleman from San Francisco, who kept quietly apart from both groups, was marked out at once. He and his ladies were hastily assisted from the car, men ran in front to show them the way, and they set off on foot, surrounded by urchins and by the sturdy Capri women who carry on their heads the luggage of decent travellers. Across the piazza, that looked like an opera scene in the light of the electric globe that swung aloft in the damp wind, clacked the wooden pattens of the women-porters. The gang of urchins began to whistle to the Gentleman from San Francisco, and to turn somersaults around him, whilst he, as if on the stage, marched among them towards a mediæval archway and under huddled houses, behind which led a little echoing lane, past tufts of palm-trees showing above the flat roofs to the left, and under the stars in the dark blue sky, upwards towards the shining entrance of the hotel.... And again it seemed as if purely in honour of the guests from San Francisco the damp little town on the rocky little island of the Mediterranean had revived from its evening stupor, that their arrival alone had made the hotel proprietor so happy and hearty, and that for them had been waiting the Chinese gong which sent its howlings through all the house the moment they crossed the doorstep.

The sight of the proprietor, a superbly elegant young man with a polite and exquisite bow, startled for a moment the Gentleman from San Francisco. In the first flash, he remembered that amid the chaos of images which had possessed him the previous night in his sleep, he had seen that very man, to a *t* the same man, in the same full-skirted frock-coat and with the same glossy, perfectly smoothed hair. Startled, he hesitated for a second. But long, long ago he had lost the last mustard-seed of any mystical feeling he might ever have had, and his surprise at once faded. He told the curious coincidence of dream and reality jestingly to his wife and daughter, as they passed along the hotel corridor. And only his daughter glanced at him with a little alarm. Her heart suddenly contracted with home-sickness, with such a violent feeling of loneliness in this dark, foreign island, that she nearly wept. As usual, however, she did not mention her feelings to her father.

Reuss XVII., a high personage who had spent three whole weeks on Capri, had just left, and the visitors were installed in the suite of rooms that he had occupied. To them was assigned the most beautiful and expert chambermaid, a Belgian with a thin, firmly corseted figure, and a starched cap in the shape of a tiny indented crown. The most experienced and distinguished-looking footman was placed at their service, a coal-black, fiery-eyed Sicilian, and also the smartest waiter, the small, stout Luigi, a tremendous buffoon, who had seen a good deal of life. In a minute or two a gentle tap was heard at the door of the Gentleman from San Francisco, and there stood the *maître d'hôtel*, a Frenchman, who had come to ask if the guests would take dinner, and to report, in case of answer in the affirmative--of which, however, he had small doubt--that this evening there were Mediterranean lobsters, roast beef, asparagus, pheasants, etc., etc. The floor was still rocking under the feet of the Gentleman from San Francisco, so rolled about had he been on that wretched, grubby Italian steamer. Yet with his own hands, calmly, though clumsily from lack of experience, he closed the window which had banged at the entrance of the *maître d'hôtel*, shutting out the drifting smell of distant kitchens and of wet flowers in the garden. Then he turned and replied with unhurried distinctness, that they would take dinner, that their table must be far from the door, in the very centre of the dining-room, that they would have local wine and champagne, moderately dry and slightly cooled. To all of which the *maître d'hôtel* gave assent in the most varied intonations, which conveyed that there was not and could not be the faintest question of the justness of the desires of the Gentleman from San Francisco, and that everything should be exactly as he wished. At the end he inclined his head and politely inquired:

"Is that all, sir?"

On receiving a lingering "Yes," he added that Carmela and Giuseppe, famous all over Italy and "to all the world of tourists," were going to dance the tarantella that evening in the hall.

"I have seen picture-postcards of her," said the Gentleman from San Francisco, in a voice expressive of nothing. "And is Giuseppe her husband?"

"Her cousin, sir," replied the *maître d'hôtel*.

The Gentleman from San Francisco was silent for a while, thinking of something, but saying nothing; then he dismissed the man with a nod of the head. After which he began to make preparations as if for his wedding. He turned on all the electric lights, and filled the mirrors with brilliance and reflection of furniture and open trunks. He began to shave and wash, ringing the bell every minute, and down the corridor raced and crossed the impatient ringings from the rooms of his wife and daughter. Luigi, with the nimbleness peculiar to certain stout people, making grimaces of horror which brought tears of laughter to the eyes of chambermaids dashing past with marble-white pails, turned a cart-wheel to the gentleman's door, and tapping with his knuckles, in a voice of sham timidity and respectfulness reduced to idiocy, asked:

"Ha suonato, Signore?"

From behind the door, a slow, grating, offensively polite voice:

"Yes, come in."

What were the feelings, what were the thoughts of the Gentleman from San Francisco on that evening so significant to him? He felt nothing exceptional, since unfortunately everything on this earth is too simple in appearance. Even had he felt something imminent in his soul, all the same he would have reasoned that, whatever it might be, it could not take place immediately. Besides, as with all who have just experienced sea-sickness, he was very hungry, and looked forward with delight to the first spoonful of soup, the first mouthful of wine. So he performed the customary business of dressing in a state of excitement which left no room for reflection.

Having shaved, washed, and dexterously arranged several artificial teeth, standing in front of the mirror, he moistened his silver-mounted brushes and plastered the remains of his thick pearly hair on his swarthy yellow skull. He drew on to his strong old body, with its abdomen protuberant from excessive good living, his cream-coloured silk underwear, put black silk socks and patent-leather slippers on his flat-footed feet. He put sleeve-links in the shining cuffs of his snow-white shirt, and bending forward so that his shirt front bulged out, he arranged his trousers that were pulled up high by his silk braces, and began to torture himself, putting his collar-stud through the stiff collar. The floor was still rocking beneath him, the tips of his fingers hurt, the stud at moments pinched the flabby skin in the recess under his Adam's apple, but he persisted, and at last, with eyes all strained and face dove-blue from the over-tight collar that enclosed his throat, he finished the business and sat down exhausted in front of the pier glass, which reflected the whole of him, and repeated him in all the other mirrors.

"It is awful!" he muttered, dropping his strong, bald head, but without trying to understand or to know what was awful. Then, with habitual careful attention examining his gouty-jointed short fingers and large, convex, almond-shaped finger-nails, he repeated: "It is awful...."

As if from a pagan temple shrilly resounded the second gong through the hotel. The Gentleman from San Francisco got up hastily, pulled his shirt-collar still tighter with his tie, and his abdomen tighter with his open waistcoat, settled his cuffs and again examined himself in the mirror...."That Carmela, swarthy, with her enticing eyes, looking like a mulatto in her dazzling-coloured dress, chiefly orange, she must be an extraordinary dancer——" he was thinking. So, cheerfully leaving his room and walking on the carpet to his wife's room, he called to ask if they were nearly ready.

"In five minutes, Dad," came the gay voice of the girl from behind the door. "I'm arranging my hair."

"Right-o!" said the Gentleman from San Francisco.

Imagining to himself her long hair hanging to the floor, he slowly walked along the corridors and staircases covered with red carpet, downstairs, looking for the reading-room. The servants he encountered on the way pressed close to the wall, and he walked past as if not noticing them. An old lady, late for dinner, already stooping with age, with milk-white hair and yet *decolletée* in her pale grey silk dress, hurried at top speed, funnily, henlike, and he easily overtook her. By the glass-door of the dining-room, wherein the guests had already started the meal, he stopped before a little table heaped with boxes of cigars and cigarettes, and taking a large Manilla, threw three liras on the table. After which he passed along the winter terrace, and glanced through an open window. From the darkness came a waft of soft air, and there loomed the top of an old palm-tree that spread its boughs over the stars, looking like a giant, bringing down the far-off smooth quivering of the sea....In the reading-room, cosy with the shaded reading-lamps, a grey, untidy German, looking rather like Ibsen in his round silver-rimmed spectacles and with mad astonished eyes, stood rustling the newspapers. After coldly eyeing him, the Gentleman from San Francisco seated himself in a deep leather armchair in a corner, by a lamp with a green shade, put on his pince-nez, and, with a stretch of his neck because of the tightness of his shirt-collar, obliterated himself behind a newspaper. He glanced over the headlines, read a few sentences about the never-ending Balkan war, then with a habitual movement turned over the page of the newspaper--when suddenly the lines blazed up before him in a glassy sheen, his neck swelled, his eyes bulged, and the pince-nez came flying off his nose....He lunged forward, wanted to breathe--and rattled wildly. His lower jaw dropped, and his mouth shone with gold fillings. His head fell swaying on his shoulder, his shirt-front bulged out basket-like, and all his body, writhing, with heels scraping up the carpet, slid down to the floor, struggling desperately with some invisible foe.

If the German had not been in the reading-room, the frightful affair could have been hushed up. Instantly, through obscure passages the Gentleman from San Francisco could have been hurried away to some dark corner, and not a single guest would have discovered what he had been up to. But the German dashed out of the room with a yell, alarming the house and all the diners. Many sprang up from the table, upsetting their chairs, many, pallid, ran towards the reading-room, and in every language it was asked: "What--what's the matter?" None answered intelligibly, nobody understood, for even to-day people are more surprised at death than at anything else, and never want to believe it is true. The proprietor rushed from one guest to another, trying to keep back those who were hastening up, to soothe them with assurances that it was a mere trifle, a fainting-fit that had overcome a certain Gentleman from San Francisco....But no one heeded him. Many saw how the porters and waiters were tearing off the tie, waistcoat, and crumpled dress-coat from that same gentleman, even, for some reason or other, pulling off his patent evening-shoes from his black-silk, flat-footed feet. And he was still writhing. He continued to struggle with death, by no means wanting to yield to that which had so unexpectedly and rudely overtaken him. He rolled his head, rattled like one throttled, and turned up the whites of his eyes as if he were drunk. When he had been hastily carried into room No. 43, the smallest, wretchedest, dampest, and coldest room at the end of the bottom corridor, his daughter came running with her hair all loose, her dressing-gown flying open, showing her bosom raised by her corsets: then his wife, large and heavy and completely dressed for dinner, her mouth opened round with terror. But by that time he had already ceased rolling his head.

In a quarter of an hour the hotel settled down somehow or other. But the evening was ruined. The guests, returning to the dining-room, finished their dinner in silence, with a look of injury on their faces, whilst the proprietor went from one to another, shrugging his shoulders in hopeless and natural irritation, feeling himself guilty through no fault of his own, assuring everybody that he perfectly realized "how disagreeable this is," and giving his word that he would take "every possible measure within his power" to remove the trouble. The tarantella had to be cancelled, the superfluous lights were switched off, most of the guests went to the bar, and soon the house became so quiet that the ticking of the clock was heard distinctly in the hall, where the lonely parrot woodenly muttered something as he bustled about in his cage preparatory to going to sleep, and managed to fall asleep at length with his paw absurdly suspended from the little upper perch.... The Gentleman from San Francisco lay on a cheap iron bed under coarse blankets on to which fell a dim light from the obscure electric lamp in the ceiling. An ice-bag slid down on his wet, cold forehead; his blue, already lifeless face grew gradually cold; the hoarse bubbling which came from his open mouth, where the gleam of gold still showed, grew weak. The Gentleman from San Francisco rattled no longer; he was no more--something else lay in his place. His wife, his daughter, the doctor, and the servants stood and watched him dully. Suddenly that which they feared and expected happened. The rattling ceased. And slowly, slowly under their eyes a pallor spread over the face of the deceased, his features began to grow thinner, more transparent ... with a beauty which might have suited him long ago....

Entered the proprietor. "Gia, e morto!" whispered the doctor to him. The proprietor raised his shoulders, as if it were not his affair. The wife, on whose cheeks tears were slowly trickling, approached and timidly asked that the deceased should be taken to his own room.

"Oh no, madame," hastily replied the proprietor, politely, but coldly, and not in English, but in French. He was no longer interested in the trifling sum the guests from San Francisco would leave at his cash desk. "That is absolutely impossible." Adding by way of explanation, that he valued that suite of rooms highly, and that should he accede to madame's request, the news would be known all over Capri and no one would take the suite afterwards.

The young lady, who had glanced at him strangely all the time, now sat down in a chair and sobbed, with her handkerchief to her mouth. The elder lady's tears dried at once, her face flared up. Raising her voice and using her own language she began to insist, unable to believe that the respect for them had gone already. The manager cut her short with polite dignity. "If madame does not like the ways of the hotel, he dare not detain her." And he announced decisively that the corpse must be removed at dawn: the police had already been notified, and an official would arrive presently to attend to the necessary formalities. "Is it possible to get a plain coffin?" madame asked. Unfortunately not! Impossible! And there was no time to make one. It would have to be arranged somehow. Yes, the English soda-water came in large strong boxes--if the divisions were removed.

The whole hotel was asleep. The window of No. 43 was open, on to a corner of the garden where, under a high stone wall ridged with broken glass, grew a battered banana tree. The light was turned off, the door locked, the room deserted. The deceased remained in the darkness, blue stars glanced at him from the black sky, a cricket started to chirp with sad carelessness in the wall.... Out in the dimly-lit corridor two chambermaids were seated in a window-sill, mending something. Entered Luigi, in slippers, with a heap of clothes in his hand.

"Pronto?" he asked, in a singing whisper, indicating with his eyes the dreadful door at the end of the corridor. Then giving a slight wave thither with his free hand: "Patenza!" he shouted in a whisper, as though sending off a train. The chambermaids, choking with noiseless laughter, dropped their heads on each other's shoulders.

Tip-toeing, Luigi went to the very door, tapped, and cocking his head on one side asked respectfully, in a subdued tone:

"Ha suonato, Signore?"

Then contracting his throat and shoving out his jaw, he answered himself in a grating, drawling, mournful voice, which seemed to come from behind the door:

"Yes, come in...."

When the dawn grew white at the window of No. 43, and a damp wind began rustling the tattered fronds of the banana tree; as the blue sky of morning lifted and unfolded over Capri, and Monte Solaro, pure and distinct, grew golden, catching the sun which was rising beyond the far-off blue mountains of Italy; just as the labourers who were mending the paths of the islands for the tourists came out for work, a long box was carried into room No. 43. Soon this box weighed heavily, and it painfully pressed the knees of the porter who was carrying it in a one-horse cab down the winding white high-road, between stone walls and vineyards, down,

down the face of Capri to the sea. The driver, a weakly little fellow with reddened eyes, in a little old jacket with sleeves too short and bursting boots, kept flogging his wiry small horse that was decorated in Sicilian fashion, its harness tinkling with busy little bells and fringed with fringes of scarlet wool, the high saddle-peak gleaming with copper and tufted with colour, and a yard-long plume nodding from the pony's cropped head, from between the ears. The cabby had spent the whole night playing dice in the inn, and was still under the effects of drink. Silent, he was depressed by his own debauchery and vice: by the fact that he gambled away to the last farthing all those copper coins with which his pockets had yesterday been full, in all four lire, forty centesimi. But the morning was fresh. In such air, with the sea all round, under the morning sky headaches evaporate, and man soon regains his cheerfulness. Moreover, the cabby was cheered by this unexpected fare which he was making out of some Gentleman from San Francisco, who was nodding with his dead head in a box at the back. The little steamer, which lay like a water-beetle on the tender bright blueness which brims the bay of Naples, was already giving the final hoots, and this tooting resounded again cheerily all over the island. Each contour, each ridge, each rock was so clearly visible in every direction, it was as if there were no atmosphere at all. Near the beach the porter in the cab was overtaken by the head porter dashing down in an automobile with the lady and her daughter, both pale, their eyes swollen with the tears of a sleepless night....And in ten minutes the little steamer again churned up the water and made her way back to Sorrento, to Castellamare, bearing away from Capri for ever the family from San Francisco....And peace and tranquillity reigned once more on the island.

On that island two thousand years ago lived a man entangled in his own infamous and strange acts, one whose rule for some reason extended over millions of people, and who, having lost his head through the absurdity of such power, committed deeds which have established him for ever in the memory of mankind; mankind which in the mass now rules the world just as hideously and incomprehensibly as he ruled it then. And men come here from all quarters of the globe to look at the ruins of the stone house where that one man lived, on the brink of one of the steepest cliffs in the island. On this exquisite morning all who had come to Capri for that purpose were still asleep in the hotels, although through the streets already trotted little mouse-coloured donkeys with red saddles, towards the hotel entrances where they would wait patiently until, after a good sleep and a square meal, young and old American men and women, German men and women would emerge and be hoisted up into the saddles, to be followed up the stony paths, yea to the very summit of Monte Tiberio, by old persistent beggar-women of Capri, with sticks in their sinewy hands. Quieted by the fact that the dead old Gentleman from San Francisco, who had intended to be one of the pleasure party but who had only succeeded in frightening the rest with the reminder of death, was now being shipped to Naples, the happy tourists still slept soundly, the island was still quiet, the shops in the little town not yet open. Only fish and greens were being sold in the tiny piazza, only simple folk were present, and amongst them, as usual without occupation, the tall old boatman Lorenzo, thorough debauchee and handsome figure, famous all over Italy, model for many a picture. He had already sold for a trifle two lobsters which he had caught in the night, and which were rustling in the apron of the cook of that very same hotel where the family from San Francisco had spent the night. And now Lorenzo could stand calmly till evening, with a majestic air showing off his rags and gazing round, holding his clay pipe with its long reed mouth-piece in his hand, and letting his scarlet bonnet slip over one ear. For as a matter of fact he received a salary from the little town, from the commune which found it profitable to pay him to stand about and make a picturesque figure--as everybody knows....Down the precipices of Monte Solaro, down the stony little stairs cut in the rock of the old Phœnician road came two Abruzzi mountaineers, descending from Anacapri. One carried a bagpipe under his leather cloak, a large goat skin with two little pipes; the other had a sort of wooden flute. They descended, and the whole land, joyous, was sunny beneath them. They saw the rocky, heaving shoulder of the island, which lay almost entirely at their feet, swimming in the fairy blueness of the water. Shining morning vapours rose over the sea to the east, under a dazzling sun which already burned hot as it rose higher and higher; and there, far off, the dimly cerulean masses of Italy, of her near and far mountains, still wavered blue as if in the world's morning, in a beauty no words can express....Halfway down the descent the pipers slackened their pace. Above the road, in a grotto of the rocky face of Monte Solaro stood the Mother of God, the sun full upon her, giving her a splendour of snow-white and blue raiment, and royal crown rusty from all weathers. Meek and merciful, she raised her eyes to heaven, to the eternal and blessed mansions of her thrice-holy Son. The pipers bared their heads, put their pipes to their lips: and there streamed forth naive and meekly joyous praises to the sun, to the morning, to Her, Immaculate, who would intercede for all who suffer in this malicious and lovely world, and to Him, born of Her womb among the caves of Bethlehem, in a lowly shepherd's hut, in the far Judean land....

And the body of the dead old man from San Francisco was returning home, to its grave, to the shores of the New World. Having been subjected to many humiliations, much human neglect, after a week's wandering from one warehouse to another, it was carried at last on to the same renowned vessel which so short a time ago, and with such honour, had borne him living to the Old World. But now he was to be hidden far from the knowledge of the voyagers. Closed in a tar-coated coffin, he was lowered deep into the vessel's dark hold. And again, again the ship set out on the long voyage. She passed at night near Capri, and to those who were looking out from the island, sad seemed the lights of the ship slowly hiding themselves in the sea's darkness. But there aboard the liner, in the bright halls shining with lights and marble, gay dancing filled the evening, as usual....

The second evening, and the third evening, still they danced, amid a storm that swept over the ocean, booming like a funeral service, rolling up mountains of mourning darkness silvered with foam. Through the snow the numerous fiery eyes of the ship were hardly visible to the Devil who watched from the rocks of Gibraltar, from the stony gateway of two worlds, peering after the vessel as she disappeared into the night and storm. The Devil was huge as a cliff. But huger still was the liner, many storeyed, many funnelled, created by the presumption of the New Man with the old heart. The blizzard smote the rigging and the funnels, and whitened the ship with snow, but she was enduring, firm, majestic--and horrible. On the topmost deck rose lonely amongst the snowy whirlwind the cosy and dim quarters where lay the heavy master of the ship, he who was like a pagan idol, sunk now in a light, uneasy slumber. Through his sleep he heard the sombre howl and furious screechings of the siren, muffled by the blizzard. But again he reassured himself by the nearness of that which stood behind his wall, and was in the last resort incomprehensible to him: by the large, apparently armoured cabin which was now and then filled with a mysterious rumbling, throbbing, and crackling of blue fires that flared up explosive around the pale face of the telegraphist who, with a metal hoop fixed on his head, was eagerly straining to catch the dim voices of vessels which spoke to him from hundreds of miles away. In the depths, in the under-water womb of the *Atlantis*, steel glimmered and steam wheezed, and huge masses of machinery and thousand-ton boilers dripped with water and oil, as the motion of the ship was steadily cooked in this vast kitchen heated by hellish furnaces from beneath. Here bubbled in their awful concentration the powers which were being transmitted to the keel, down an infinitely long round tunnel lit up and brilliant like a gigantic gun-barrel, along which slowly, with a regularity crushing to the human soul, revolved a gigantic shaft, precisely like a living monster coiling and uncoiling its endless length down the tunnel, sliding on its bed of oil. The middle of the *Atlantis*, the warm, luxurious cabins, dining-rooms, halls, shed light and joy, buzzed with the chatter of an elegant crowd, was fragrant with fresh flowers, and quivered with the sounds of a string orchestra. And again amidst that crowd, amidst the brilliance of lights, silks, diamonds, and bare feminine shoulders, a slim and supple pair of hired lovers painfully writhed and at moments convulsively clashed. A sinfully discreet, pretty girl with lowered lashes and hair innocently dressed, and a tallish young man with black hair looking as if it were glued on, pale with powder, and wearing the most elegant patent-leather shoes and a narrow, long-tailed dress coat, a beau resembling an enormous leech. And no one knew that this couple had long since grown weary of shamly tormenting themselves with their beatific love-tortures, to the sound of bawdy-sad music; nor did any one know of that thing which lay deep, deep below at the very bottom of the dark hold, near the gloomy and sultry bowels of the ship that was so gravely overcoming the darkness, the ocean, the blizzard....

GENTLE BREATHING

In the cemetery above a fresh mound of earth stands a new cross of oak--strong, heavy, smooth, a pleasant thing to look at. It is April, but the days are grey. From a long way off one can see through the bare trees the tomb-stones in the cemetery--a spacious, real country or cathedral town cemetery; the cold wind goes whistling, whistling through the china wreath at the foot of the cross. In the cross itself is set a rather large bronze medallion, and in the medallion is a portrait of a smart and charming school-girl, with happy, astonishingly vivacious eyes.

It is Olga Meschersky.

As a little girl there was nothing to distinguish her in the noisy crowd of brown dresses which made its discordant and youthful hum in the corridors and class-rooms; all that one could say of her was that she was just one of a number of pretty, rich, happy little girls, that she was clever, but playful, and very careless of the precepts of her class-teacher. Then she began to develop and to blossom, not by days, but by hours. At fourteen, with a slim waist and graceful legs, there was already well developed the outline of her breasts and all those contours of which the charm has never yet been expressed in human words; at fifteen she was said to be a beauty. How carefully some of her school friends did their hair, how clean they were, how careful and restrained in their movements! But she was afraid of nothing--neither of ink-stains on her fingers, nor of a flushed face, nor of dishevelled hair, nor of a bare knee after a rush and a tumble. Without a thought or an effort on her part, imperceptibly there came to her everything which so distinguished her from the rest of the school during her last two years--daintiness, smartness, quickness, the bright and intelligent gleam in her eyes. No one danced like Olga Meschersky, no one could run or skate like her, no one at dances had as many admirers as she had, and for some reason no one was so popular with the junior classes. Imperceptibly she grew up into a girl and imperceptibly her fame in the school became established, and already there were rumours that she is flighty, that she cannot live without admirers, that the schoolboy, Shensin, is madly in love with her, that she, too, perhaps loves him, but is so changeable in her treatment of him that he tried to commit suicide....

During her last winter, Olga Meschersky went quite crazy with happiness, so they said at school. It was a snowy, sunny, frosty winter; the sun would go down early behind the grove of tall fir-trees in the snowy school garden; but it was always fine and radiant weather, with a promise of frost and sun again to-morrow, a walk in Cathedral Street, skating in the town park, a pink sunset, music, and that perpetually moving crowd in which Olga Meschersky seemed to be the smartest, the most careless, and the happiest. And then, one day, when she was rushing like a whirlwind through the recreation room with the little girls chasing her and screaming for joy, she was unexpectedly called up to the headmistress. She stopped short, took one deep breath, with a quick movement, already a habit, arranged her hair, gave a pull to the corners of her apron to bring it up on her shoulders, and with shining eyes ran upstairs. The headmistress, small, youngish, but grey-haired, sat quietly with her knitting in her hands at the writing-table, under the portrait of the Tsar.

"Good morning, Miss Meschersky," she said in French, without lifting her eyes from her knitting. "I am sorry that this is not the first time that I have had to call you here to speak to you about your behaviour."

"I am attending, madam," answered Olga, coming up to the table, looking at her brightly and happily, but with an expressionless face, and curtsying so lightly and gracefully, as only she could.

"You will attend badly--unfortunately I have become convinced of that," said the headmistress, giving a pull at the thread so that the ball rolled away over the polished floor, and Olga watched it with curiosity. The headmistress raised her eyes: "I shall not repeat myself, I shall not say much," she said.

Olga very much liked the unusually clean and large study; on frosty days the air in it was so pleasant with the warmth from the shining Dutch fire-place, and the fresh lilies-of-the-valley on the writing-table. She glanced at the young Tsar, painted full-length in a splendid hall, at the smooth parting in the white, neatly waved hair of the headmistress; she waited in silence.

"You are no longer a little girl," said the headmistress meaningly, beginning to feel secretly irritated.

"Yes, madam," answered Olga simply, almost merrily.

"But neither are you a woman yet," said the headmistress, still more meaningly, and her pale face flushed a little. "To begin with, why do you do your hair like that? You do it like a woman."

"It is not my fault, madam, that I have nice hair," Olga replied, and gave a little touch with both hands to her beautifully dressed hair.

"Ah, is that it? You are not to blame!" said the headmistress. "You are not to blame for the way you do your hair; you are not to blame for those expensive combs; you are not to blame for ruining your parents with your twenty-rouble shoes. But, I repeat, you completely forget that you are still only a schoolgirl...."

And here Olga, without losing her simplicity and calm, suddenly interrupted her politely:

"Excuse me, madam, you are mistaken--I am a woman. And, do you know who is to blame for that? My father's friend and neighbour, your brother, Alexey Mikhailovitch Malyntin. It happened last summer in the country...."

And a month after this conversation, a Cossack officer, ungainly and of plebeian appearance, who had absolutely nothing in common with Olga Meschersky's circle, shot her on the platform of the railway station, in a large crowd of people who had just arrived by train. And the incredible confession of Olga Meschersky, which had stunned the headmistress, was completely confirmed; the officer told the coroner that Meschersky had led him on, had had a *liaison* with him, had promised to marry him, and at the railway station on the day of the murder, while seeing him off to Novocherkask had suddenly told him that she had never thought of marrying him, that all the talk about marriage was only to make a fool of him, and she gave him her diary to read with the pages in it which told about Malyntin.

"I glanced through those pages," said the officer, "went out on to the platform where she was walking up and down, and waiting for me to finish reading it, and I shot her. The diary is in the pocket of my overcoat; look at the entry for July 10 of last year."

And this is what the coroner read:

"It is now nearly two o'clock in the morning. I fell sound asleep, but woke up again immediately....I have become a woman to-day! Papa, mamma, and Tolya had all gone to town, and I was left alone. I cannot say how happy I was to be alone. In the morning I walked in the orchard, in the field, and I went into the woods, and it seemed to me that I was all by myself in the whole world, and I never had such pleasant thoughts before. I had lunch by myself; then I played for an hour, and the music made me feel that I should live for ever, and be happier than any one else had ever been. Then I fell asleep in papa's study, and at four o'clock Kate woke me, and said that Alexey Mikhailovitch had come. I was very glad to see him; it was so pleasant to receive him and entertain him. He came with his pair of Viatka horses, very beautiful, and they stood all the time at the front door, but he stayed because it was raining, and hoped that the roads would dry towards evening. He was very sorry not to find papa at home, was very animated and treated me very politely, and made many jokes about his having been long in love with me. Before tea we walked in the garden, and the weather was charming, the sun shining through the whole wet garden; but it grew quite cold, and he walked with me, arm in arm, and said that he was Faust with Margarete. He is fifty-six, but still very handsome, and always very well dressed--the only thing I didn't like was his coming in a sort of cape--he smells of English eau-de-Cologne, and his eyes are quite young, black; his beard is long and elegantly parted down the middle, it is quite silvery. We had tea in the glass verandah, and suddenly I did not feel very well, and lay down on the sofa while he smoked; then he sat down near me, and began to say nice things, and then to take my hand and kiss it. I covered my face with a silk handkerchief, and several times he kissed me on the lips through the handkerchief.... I can't understand how it happened; I went mad; I never thought I was like that. Now I have only one way out.... I feel such a loathing for him that I cannot endure it...."

The town in these April days has become clean and dry, its stones have become white, and it is easy and pleasant to walk on them. Every Sunday, after mass, along Cathedral Street which leads out of the town, there walks a little woman in mourning, in black kid gloves, and with an ebony sunshade. She crosses the yard of the fire-station, crosses the dirty market-place by the road where there are many black smithies, and where the wind blows fresher from the fields; in the distance, between the monastery and the gaol, is the white slope of the sky and the grey of the spring fields; and then, when you have passed the muddy pools behind the monastery wall and turn to the left, you will see what looks like a large low garden, surrounded by a white wall, on the gates of which is written "The Assumption of Our Lady." The little woman makes rapid little signs of the cross, and always walks on the main path. When she gets to the bench opposite the oak cross she sits down, in the wind and the chilly spring, for an hour, two hours, until her feet in the light boots, and her hand in the narrow kid glove, grow quite cold. Listening to the birds of spring, singing sweetly even in the cold, listening to the whistling of the wind through the porcelain wreath, she sometimes thinks that she would give half her life if only that dead wreath might not be before her eyes. The thought that it is Olga Meschersky who has been buried in that clay plunges her into astonishment bordering upon stupidity: how can one associate the sixteen-year-old school-girl, who but two or three months ago was so full of life, charm, happiness, with that mound of earth and that oak cross. Is it possible that beneath it is the same girl whose eyes shine out immortally from this bronze medallion, and how can one connect this bright look with the horrible event which is associated now with Olga Meschersky? But in the depths of her soul the little woman is happy, as are all those who are in love or are generally devoted to some passionate dream.

The woman is Olga Meschersky's class-mistress, a girl over thirty, who has for long been living on some illusion and putting it in the place of her actual life. At first the illusion was her brother, a poor lieutenant, in no way remarkable--her whole soul was bound up in him and in his future, which, for some reason, she imagined as splendid, and she lived in the curious expectation that, thanks to him, her fate would transport her into some fairyland. Then, when he was killed at Mukden, she persuaded herself that she, very happily, is not like others, that instead of beauty and womanliness she has intellect and higher interests, that she is a worker for the ideal. And now Olga Meschersky is the object of all her thoughts, of her admiration and joy. Every holiday she goes to her grave--she had formed the habit of going to the cemetery after the death of her brother--for hours she never takes her eyes off the oak cross; she recalls Olga Meschersky's pale face in the coffin amid the flowers, and remembers what she once overheard: once during the luncheon hour, while walking in the school garden, Olga Meschersky was quickly, quickly saying to her favourite friend, the tall plump Subbotin:

"I have been reading one of papa's books--he has a lot of funny old books--I read about the kind of beauty which woman ought to possess. There's such a lot written there, you see, I can't remember it all; well, of course, eyes black as boiling pitch--upon my word, that's what they say there, boiling pitch!--eye-brows black as night, and a tender flush in the complexion, a slim figure, hands longer than the ordinary--little feet, a fairly large breast, a regularly rounded leg, a knee the colour of the inside of a shell, high but sloping shoulders--a good deal of it I have nearly learnt by heart, it is all so true; but do you know what the chief thing is? Gentle breathing! And I have got it; you listen how I breathe; isn't it gentle?"

Now the gentle breathing has again vanished away into the world, into the cloudy day, into the cold spring wind....

KASIMIR STANISLAVOVITCH

On the yellow card with a nobleman's coronet the young porter at the Hotel "Versailles" somehow managed to read the Christian name and patronymic "Kasimir Stanislavovitch."[1] There followed something still more complicated and still more difficult to pronounce. The porter turned the card this way and that way in his hand, looked at the passport, which the visitor had given him with it, shrugged his shoulders--none of those who stayed at the "Versailles" gave their cards--then he threw both on to the table and began again to examine himself in the silvery, milky mirror which hung above the table, whipping up his thick hair with a comb. He wore an overcoat and shiny top-boots; the gold braid on his cap was greasy with age--the hotel was a bad one.

Kasimir Stanislavovitch left Kiev for Moscow on April 8th, Good Friday, on receiving a telegram with the one word "tenth." Somehow or other he managed to get the money for his fare, and took his seat in a second-class compartment, grey and dim, but really giving him the sensation of comfort and luxury. The train was heated, and that railway-carriage heat and the smell of the heating apparatus, and the sharp tapping of the little hammers in it, reminded Kasimir Stanislavovitch of other times. At times it seemed to him that winter had returned, that in the fields the white, very white drifts of snow had covered up the yellowish bristle of stubble and the large leaden pools where the wild-duck swam. But often the snow-storm stopped suddenly and melted; the fields grew bright, and one felt that behind the clouds was much light, and the wet platforms of the railway-stations looked black, and the rooks called from the naked poplars. At each big station Kasimir Stanislavovitch went to the refreshment-room for a drink, and returned to his carriage with newspapers in his hands; but he did not read them; he only sat and sank in the thick smoke of his cigarettes, which burned and glowed, and to none of his neighbours--Odessa Jews who played cards all the time--did he say a single word. He wore an autumn overcoat of which the pockets were worn, a very old black top-hat, and new, but heavy, cheap boots. His hands, the typical hands of an habitual drunkard, and an old inhabitant of basements, shook when he lit a match. Everything else about him spoke of poverty and drunkenness: no cuffs, a dirty linen collar, an ancient tie, an inflamed and ravaged face, bright-blue watery eyes. His side-whiskers, dyed with a bad, brown dye, had an unnatural appearance. He looked tired and contemptuous.

The train reached Moscow next day, not at all up to time; it was seven hours late. The weather was neither one thing nor the other, but better and drier than in Kiev, with something stirring in the air. Kasimir Stanislavovitch took a cab without bargaining with the driver, and told him to drive straight to the "Versailles." "I have known that hotel, my good fellow," he said, suddenly breaking his silence, "since my student days." From the "Versailles," as soon as his little bag, tied with stout rope, had been taken up to his room, he immediately went out.

It was nearly evening: the air was warm, the black trees on the boulevards were turning green; everywhere there were crowds of people, cars, carts. Moscow was trafficking and doing business, was returning to the usual, pressing work, was ending her holiday, and unconsciously welcomed the spring. A man who has lived his life and ruined it feels lonely on a spring evening in a strange, crowded city. Kasimir Stanislavovitch walked the whole length of the Tverskoy Boulevard; he saw once more the cast-iron figure of the musing Poushkin, the golden and lilac top of the Strasnoy Monastery....For about an hour he sat at the Café Filippov, drank chocolate, and read old comic papers. Then he went to a cinema, whose flaming signs shone from far away down the Tverskaya, through the darkling twilight. From the cinema he drove to a restaurant on the boulevard which he had also known in his student days. He was driven by an old man, bent in a bow, sad, gloomy, deeply absorbed in himself, in his old age, in his dark thoughts. All the way the man painfully and wearily helped on his lazy horse with his whole being, murmuring something to it all the time and occasionally bitterly reproaching it--and at last, when he reached the place, he allowed the load to slip from his shoulders for a moment and gave a deep sigh, as he took the money.

"I did not catch the name, and thought you meant 'Brague'!" he muttered, turning his horse slowly; he seemed displeased, although the "Prague" was further away.

"I remember the 'Prague' too, old fellow," answered Kasimir Stanislavovitch. "You must have been driving for a long time in Moscow."

"Driving?" the old man said; "I have been driving now for fifty-one years."

"That means that you may have driven me before," said Kasimir Stanislavovitch.

"Perhaps I did," answered the old man dryly. "There are lots of people in the world; one can't remember all of you."

Of the old restaurant, once known to Kasimir Stanislavovitch, there remained only the name. Now it was a large, first-class, though vulgar, restaurant. Over the entrance burnt an electric globe which illuminated with its unpleasant, heliotrope light the smart, second-rate cabmen, impudent, and cruel to their lean, short-winded steeds. In the damp hall stood pots of laurels and tropical plants of the kind which one sees carried on to the platforms from weddings to funerals and *vice versa*. From the porters' lodge several men rushed out together to Kasimir Stanislavovitch, and all of them had just the same thick curl of hair as the porter at the "Versailles." In the large greenish room, decorated in the rococo style, were a multitude of broad mirrors, and in the corner burnt a crimson icon-lamp. The room was still empty, and only a few of the electric lights were on. Kasimir Stanislavovitch sat for a long time alone, doing nothing. One felt that behind the windows with their white blinds the long, spring evening had not yet grown dark; one heard from the street the thudding of hooves; in the middle of the room there was the monotonous splash-splash of the little fountain in an aquarium round which gold-fish, with their scales peeling off, lighted somehow from below, swam through the water. A waiter in white brought the dinner things, bread, and a decanter of cold vodka. Kasimir Stanislavovitch began drinking the vodka, held it in his mouth before swallowing it, and, having swallowed it, smelt the black bread as though with loathing. With a suddenness which gave even him a start, a gramophone began to roar out through the room a mixture of Russian songs, now exaggeratedly boisterous and turbulent, now too tender, drawling, sentimental.... And Kasimir Stanislavovitch's eyes grew red and tears filmed them at that sweet and snuffling drone of the machine.

Then a grey-haired, curly, black-eyed Georgian brought him, on a large iron fork, a half-cooked, smelly shashlyk, cut off the meat on to the plate with a kind of dissolute smartness, and, with Asiatic simplicity, with his own hand sprinkled it with onions, salt, and rusty barbery powder, while the gramophone roared out in the empty hall a cake-walk, inciting one to jerks and spasms. Then Kasimir Stanislavovitch was served with cheese, fruit, red wine, coffee, mineral water, liquers.... The gramophone had long ago grown silent; instead of it there had been playing on the platform an orchestra of German women dressed in white; the lighted hall, continually filling up with people, grew hot, became dim with tobacco smoke and heavily saturated with the smell of food; waiters rushed about in a whirl; drunken people ordered cigars which immediately made them sick; the head-waiters showed excessive officiousness, combined with an intense realization of their own dignity; in the mirrors, in the watery gloom of their abysses, there was more and more chaotically reflected something huge, noisy, complicated. Several times Kasimir Stanislavovitch went out of the hot hall into the cool corridors, into the cold lavatory, where there was a strange smell of the sea; he walked as if on air, and, on returning to his table, again ordered wine. After midnight, closing his eyes and drawing the fresh night air through his nostrils into his intoxicated head, he raced in a hansom-cab on rubber tyres out of the town to a brothel; he saw in the distance infinite chains of light, running away somewhere down hill and then up hill again, but he saw it just as if it were not he, but some one else, seeing it. In the brothel he nearly had a fight with a stout gentleman who attacked him shouting that he was known to all thinking Russia. Then he lay, dressed, on a broad bed, covered with a satin quilt, in a little room half-lighted from the ceiling by a sky-blue lantern, with a sickly smell of scented soap, and with dresses hanging from a hook on the door. Near the bed stood a dish of fruit, and the girl who had been hired to entertain Kasimir Stanislavovitch, silently, greedily, with relish ate a pear, cutting off slices with a knife, and her friend, with fat bare arms, dressed only in a chemise which made her look like a little girl, was rapidly writing on the toilet-table, taking no notice of them. She wrote and wept--of what? There are lots of people in the world; one can't know everything....

On the tenth of April Kasimir Stanislavovitch woke up early. Judging from the start with which he opened his eyes, one could see that he was overwhelmed by the idea that he was in Moscow. He had got back after four in the morning. He staggered down the staircase of the "Versailles," but without a mistake he went straight to his room down the long, stinking tunnel of a corridor which was lighted only at its entrance by a little lamp smoking sleepily. Outside every room stood boots and shoes--all of strangers, unknown to one another, hostile to one another. Suddenly a door opened, almost terrifying Kasimir Stanislavovitch; on its threshold appeared an old man, looking like a third-rate actor acting "The Memoirs of a Lunatic," and Kasimir Stanislavovitch saw a lamp under a green shade and a room crowded with things, the cave of a lonely, old lodger, with icons in the corner, and innumerable cigarette boxes piled one upon another almost to the ceiling, near the icons. Was that the half-crazy writer of the lives of the saints, who had lived in the "Versailles" twenty-three years ago? Kasimir Stanislavovitch's dark room was terribly hot with a malignant and smelly dryness....The light from the window over the door came faintly into the darkness. Kasimir Stanislavovitch went behind the screen, took the top-hat off his thin, greasy hair, threw his overcoat over the end of his bare bed....As soon as he lay down, everything began to turn round him, to rush into an abyss, and he fell asleep instantly. In his sleep all the time he was conscious of the smell of the iron wash-stand which stood close to his face, and he dreamt of a spring day, trees in blossom, the hall of a manor house and a number of people waiting anxiously for the bishop to arrive at any moment; and all night long he was wearied and tormented with that waiting....Now in the corridors of the "Versailles" people rang, ran, called to one another. Behind the screen, through the double, dusty window-panes, the sun shone; it was almost hot....Kasimir Stanislavovitch took off his jacket, rang the bell, and began to wash. There came in a quick-eyed boy, the page-boy, with fox-coloured hair on his head, in a frock-coat and pink shirt.

"A loaf, samovar, and lemon," Kasimir Stanislavovitch said without looking at him.

"And tea and sugar?" the boy asked with Moscow sharpness.

And a minute later he rushed in with a boiling samovar in his hand, held out level with his shoulders; on the round table in front of the sofa he quickly put a tray with a glass and a battered brass slop-basin, and thumped the samovar down on the tray....Kasimir Stanislavovitch, while the tea was drawing, mechanically opened the *Moscow Daily*, which the page-boy had brought in with the samovar. His eye fell on a report that yesterday an unknown man had been picked up unconscious...."The victim was taken to the hospital," he read, and threw the paper away. He felt very bad and unsteady. He got up and opened the window--it faced the yard--and a breath of freshness and of the city came to him; there came to him the melodious shouts of hawkers, the bells of horse-trams humming behind the house opposite, the blended rap-tap of the cars, the musical drone of church-bells....The city had long since started its huge, noisy life in that bright, jolly, almost spring day. Kasimir Stanislavovitch squeezed the lemon into a glass of tea and greedily drank the sour, muddy liquid; then he again went behind the screen. The "Versailles" was quiet. It was pleasant and peaceful; his eye wandered leisurely over the hotel notice on the wall: "A stay of three hours is reckoned as a full day." A mouse scuttled in the chest of drawers, rolling about a piece of sugar left there by some visitor....Thus half asleep Kasimir Stanislavovitch lay for a long time behind the screen, until the sun had gone from the room and another freshness was wafted in from the window, the freshness of evening.

Then he carefully got himself in order: he undid his bag, changed his underclothing, took out a cheap, but clean handkerchief, brushed his shiny frock-coat, top-hat, and overcoat, took out of its torn pocket a crumpled Kiev newspaper of January 15, and threw it away into the corner....Having dressed and combed his whiskers with a dyeing comb, he counted his money-- there remained in his purse four roubles, seventy copecks--and went out. Exactly at six o'clock he was outside a low, ancient, little church in the Molchanovka. Behind the church fence a spreading tree was just breaking into green; children were playing there--the black stocking of one thin little girl, jumping over a rope, was continually coming down--and he sat there on a bench among perambulators with sleeping babies and nurses in Russian costumes. Sparrows prattled over all the tree; the air was soft, all but summer--even the dust smelt of summer--the sky above the sunset behind the houses melted into a gentle gold, and one felt that once more there was somewhere in the world joy, youth, happiness. In the church the chandeliers were already burning, and there stood the pulpit and in front of the pulpit was spread a little carpet. Kasimir Stanislavovitch cautiously took off his top-hat, trying not to untidy his hair, and entered the church nervously; he went into a corner, but a corner from which he could see the couple to be married. He looked at the painted vault, raised his eyes to the cupola, and his every movement and every gasp echoed loudly through the silence. The church shone with gold; the candles sputtered expectantly. And now the priests and choir began to enter, crossing themselves with the carelessness which comes of habit, then old women, children, smart wedding guests, and worried stewards. A noise was heard in the porch, the crunching wheels of the carriage, and every one turned their heads towards the entrance, and the hymn burst out "Come, my dove!" Kasimir Stanislavovitch became deadly pale, as his heart beat, and unconsciously he took a step forward. And close by him there passed--her veil touching him, and a breath of lily-of-the-valley--she who did not know even of his existence in the world; she passed, bending her charming head, all flowers and transparent gauze, all snow-white and innocent, happy and timid, like a princess going to her first communion.... Kasimir Stanislavovitch hardly saw the bridegroom who came to meet her, a rather small, broad-shouldered man with yellow, close-cropped hair. During the whole ceremony only one thing was before his eyes: the bent head, in the flowers and the veil, and the little hand trembling as it held a burning candle tied with a white ribbon in a bow....

About ten o'clock he was back again in the hotel. All his overcoat smelt of the spring air. After coming out of the church, he had seen, near the porch, the car lined with white satin, and its window reflecting the sunset, and behind the window there flashed on him for the last time the face of her who was being carried away from him for ever. After that he had wandered about in little streets, and had come out on the Novensky Boulevard.... Now slowly and with trembling hands he took off his overcoat, put on the table a paper bag containing two green cucumbers which for some reason he had bought at a hawker's stall. They too smelt of spring even through the paper, and spring-like through the upper pane of the window the April moon shone silvery high up in the not yet darkened sky. Kasimir Stanislavovitch lit a candle, sadly illuminating his empty, casual home, and sat down on the sofa, feeling on his face the freshness of evening.... Thus he sat for a long time. He did not ring the bell, gave no orders, locked himself in--all this seemed suspicious to the porter who had seen him enter his room with his shuffling feet and taking the key out of the door in order to lock himself in from the inside. Several times the porter stole up on tiptoe to the door and looked through the key-hole: Kasimir Stanislavovitch was sitting on the sofa, trembling and wiping his face with a handkerchief, and weeping so bitterly, so copiously that the brown dye came off, and was smeared over his face.

At night he tore the cord off the blind, and, seeing nothing through his tears, began to fasten it to the hook of the clothes-peg. But the guttering candle flickered and the paper bag, and terrible dark waves swam and flickered over the locked room: he was old, weak--and he himself was well aware of it.... No, it was not in his power to die by his own hand!

In the morning he started for the railway station about three hours before the train left. At the station he quietly walked about among the passengers, with his eyes on the ground and tear-stained; and he would stop unexpectedly now before one and now before another, and in a low voice, evenly but without expression, he would say rather quickly:

"For God's sake ... I am in a desperate position.... My fare to Briansk.... If only a few copecks...."

And some passengers, trying not to look at his top-hat, at the worn velvet collar of his overcoat, at the dreadful face with the faded violet whiskers, hurriedly, and with confusion, gave him something.

And then, rushing out of the station on to the platform, he got mixed in the crowd and disappeared into it, while in the "Versailles," in the room which for two days had as it were belonged to him, they carried out the slop-pail, opened the windows to the April sun and to the fresh air, noisily moved the furniture, swept up and threw out the dust--and with the dust there fell under the table, under the table cloth which slid on to the floor, his torn note, which he had forgotten with the cucumbers:

"I beg that no one be accused of my death. I was at the wedding of my only daughter who...."

---

[1]	*I.e.* There was no family name. The name is Polish, not Russian.

SON

Madame Maraud was born and grew up in Lausanne, in a strict, honest, industrious family. She did not marry young, but she married for love. In March, 1876, among the passengers on an old French ship, the *Auvergne*, sailing from Marseilles to Italy, was the newly married couple. The weather was calm and fresh; the silvery mirror of the sea appeared and disappeared in the mists of the spring horizon. The newly married couple never left the deck. Every one liked them, every one looked at their happiness with friendly smiles; his happiness showed itself in the energy and keenness of his glance, in a need for movement, in the animation of his welcome to those around him; hers showed itself in the joy and interest with which she took in each detail.... The newly married couple were the Marauds.

He was about ten years her elder; he was not tall, with a swarthy face and curly hair; his hand was dry and his voice melodious. One felt in her the presence of some other, non-Latin blood; she was over medium height, although her figure was charming, and she had dark hair and blue-grey eyes. After touching at Naples, Palermo, and Tunis, they arrived at the Algerian town of Constantine, where M. Maraud had obtained a rather good post. And their life in Constantine, for the fourteen years since that happy spring, gave them everything with which people are normally satisfied: wealth, family happiness, healthy and beautiful children.

During the fourteen years the Marauds had greatly changed in appearance. He became as dark as an Arab; from his work, from travelling, from tobacco and the sun, he had grown grey and dried up--many people mistook him for a native of Algeria. And it would have been impossible to recognize in her the woman who sailed once in the *Auvergne*: at that time there was even in the boots which she put outside her door at night the charm of youth; now there was silver in her hair, her skin had become more transparent and more of a golden colour, her hands were thinner and in her care of them, of her linen, and of her clothes she already showed a certain excessive tidiness. Their relations had certainly changed too, although no one could say for the worse. They each lived their own life: his time was filled with work--he remained the same passionate, and, at the same time, sober man that he had been before; her time was filled up with looking after him and their children, two pretty girls, of whom the elder was almost a young lady: and every one with one voice agreed that in all Constantine there was no better hostess, no better mother, no more charming companion in the drawing-room than Madame Maraud.

Their house stood in a quiet, clean part of the town. From the front rooms on the second floor, which were always half dark with the blinds drawn down, one saw Constantine, known the world over for its picturesqueness. On steep rocks stands the ancient Arab fortress which has become a French city. The windows of the living-rooms looked into a garden where in perpetual heat and sunshine slumbered the evergreen eucalyptuses, the sycamores, and palms behind high walls. The master was frequently away on business, and the lady led the secluded existence to which the wives of Europeans are doomed in the colonies. On Sundays she always went to church. On weekdays she rarely went out, and she visited only a small and select circle. She read, did needle-work, talked or did lessons with the children; sometimes taking her younger daughter, the black-eyed Marie, on her knee, she would play the piano with one hand and sing old French songs, in order to while away the long African day, while the great breath of hot wind blew in through the open windows from the garden.... Constantine, with all its shutters closed and scorched pitilessly by the sun, seemed at such hours a dead city: only the birds called behind the garden wall, and from the hills behind the town came the dreary sound of pipes, filled with the melancholy of colonial countries, and at times there the dull thud of guns shook the earth, and you could see the flashing of the white helmets of soldiers.

The days in Constantine passed monotonously, but no one noticed that Madame Maraud minded that. In her pure, refined nature there was no trace of abnormal sensitiveness or excessive nervousness. Her health could not be called robust, but it gave no cause of anxiety to M. Maraud. Only one incident once astonished him: in Tunis once, an Arab juggler so quickly and completely hypnotized her that it was only with difficulty that she could be brought to. But this happened at the time of their arrival from France; she had never since experienced so sudden a loss of will-power, such a morbid suggestibility. And M. Maraud was happy, untroubled, convinced that her soul was tranquil and open to him. And it was so, even in the last, the fourteenth year of their married life. But then there appeared in Constantine Emile Du-Buis.

Emile Du-Buis, the son of Madame Bonnay, an old and good friend of M. Maraud, was only nineteen. Emile was the son of her first husband and had grown up in Paris where he studied law, but he spent most of his time in writing poems, intelligible only to himself; he was attached to the school of "Seekers" which has now ceased to exist. Madame Bonnay, the widow of an engineer, also had a daughter, Elise. In May, 1889, Elise was just going to be married, when she fell ill and died a few days before her wedding, and Emile, who had never been in Constantine, came to the funeral. It can be easily understood how that death moved Madame Maraud, the death of a girl already trying on her wedding dress; it is also known how quickly in such circumstances an intimacy springs up between people who have hardly met before. Besides, to Madame Maraud Emile was, indeed, only a boy. Soon after the funeral Madame Bonnay went for the summer to stay with her relations in France. Emile remained in Constantine, in a suburban villa which belonged to his late step-father, the villa "Hashim," as it was called in the town, and he began coming nearly every day to the Marauds. Whatever he was, whatever he pretended to be, he was still very young, very sensitive, and he needed people to whom he could attach himself for a time. "And isn't it strange?" some said; "Madame Maraud has become unrecognizable! How lively she has become, and how her looks have improved!"

However, these insinuations were groundless. At first there was only this, that her life had become a little bit jollier, and her girls too had become more playful and coquettish, since Emile, every now and then forgetting his sorrow and the poison with which, as he thought, the *fin de siècle* had infected him, would for hours at a time play with Marie and Louise as if he were their age. It is true that he was all the same a man, a Parisian, and not altogether an ordinary man. He had already taken part in that life, inaccessible to ordinary mortals, which Parisian writers live; he often read aloud, with a hypnotic expressiveness, strange but sonorous poems; and, perhaps it was entirely owing to him that Madame Maraud's walk had become lighter and quicker, her dress at home imperceptibly smarter, the tones of her voice more tender and playful. Perhaps, too, there was in her soul a drop of purely feminine pleasure that here was a man to whom she could give her small commands, with whom she could talk, half seriously and half jokingly as a mentor, with that freedom which their difference in age so naturally allowed--a man who was so devoted to her whole household, in which, however, the first person--this, of course, very soon became clear--was for him, nevertheless, she herself. But how common all that is! And the chief thing was that often what she really felt for him was only pity.

He honestly thought himself a born poet, and he wished outwardly too to look like a poet; his long hair was brushed back with artistic modesty; his hair was fine, brown, and suited his pale face just as did his black clothes; but the pallor was too bloodless, with a yellow tinge in it; his eyes were always shining, but the tired look in his face made them seem feverish; and so flat and narrow was his chest, so thin his legs and hands, that one felt a little uncomfortable when one saw him get very excited and run in the street or garden, with his body pushed forward a little, as though he were gliding, in order to hide his defect, that he had one leg shorter than the other. In company he was apt to be unpleasant, haughty, trying to appear mysterious, negligent, at times elegantly dashing, at times contemptuously absent-minded, in everything independent; but too often he could not carry it through to the end, he became confused and began to talk hurriedly with naïve frankness. And, of course, he was not very long able to hide his feelings, to maintain the pose of not believing in love or in happiness on earth. He had already begun to bore his host by his visits; every day he would bring from his villa bouquets of the rarest flowers, and he would sit from morn to night reading poems which were more and more unintelligible--the children often heard him beseeching some one that they should die together--while he spent his nights in the native quarter, in dens where Arabs, wrapped in dirty white robes, greedily watch the *danse de ventre*, and drank fiery liqueurs....In a word it took less than six weeks for his passion to change into God knows what.

His nerves gave way completely. Once he sat for nearly the whole day in silence; then he got up, bowed, took his hat and went out--and half an hour later he was carried in from the street in a terrible state; he was in hysterics and he wept so passionately that he terrified the children and servants. But Madame Maraud, it seemed, did not attach any particular importance to this delirium. She herself tried to help him recover himself, quickly undid his tie, told him to be a man, and she only smiled when he, without any restraint in her husband's presence, caught her hands and covered them with kisses and vowed devotion to her. But an end had to be put to all this. When, a few days after this outbreak, Emile, whom the children had greatly missed, arrived calm, but looking like some one who has been through a serious illness, Madame Maraud gently told him everything which is always said on such occasions.

"My friend, you are like a son to me," she said to him, for the first time uttering the word son, and, indeed, almost feeling a maternal affection. "Don't put me in a ridiculous and painful position."

"But I swear to you, you are mistaken!" he exclaimed, with passionate sincerity. "I am only devoted to you. I only want to see you, nothing else!"

And suddenly he fell on his knees--they were in the garden, on a quiet, hot, dark evening-- impetuously embraced her knees, nearly fainting with passion. And looking at his hair, at his thin white neck, she thought with pain and ecstasy:

"Ah yes, yes, I might have had such a son, almost his age!"

However, from that time until he left for France he behaved reasonably. This essentially was a bad sign, for it might mean that his passion had become deeper. But outwardly everything had changed for the better--only once did he break down. It was on a Sunday after dinner at which several strangers were present, and he, careless of whether they noticed it, said to her:

"I beg you to spare me a minute."

She got up and followed him into the empty, half-dark drawing-room. He went to the window through which the evening light fell in broad shafts, and, looking straight into her face, said:

"To-day is the day on which my father died. I love you!"

She turned and was about to leave him. Frightened, he hastily called after her:

"Forgive me, it is for the first and last time!"

Indeed, she heard no further confessions from him. "I was fascinated by her agitation," he noted that night in his diary in his elegant and pompous style; "I swore never again to disturb her peace of mind: am I not blessed enough without that?" He continued to come to town--he only slept at the villa Hashim--and he behaved erratically, but always more or less properly. At times he was, as before, unnaturally playful and naïve, running about with the children in the garden; but more often he sat with her and "sipped of her presence," read newspapers and novels to her, and "was happy in her listening to him." "The children were not in the way," he wrote of those days, "their voices, laughter, comings and goings, their very beings acted like the subtlest conductors for our feelings; thanks to them, the charm of those feelings was intensified; we talked about the most everyday matters, but something else sounded through what we said: our happiness; yes, yes, she, too, was happy--I maintain that! She loved me to read poetry; in the evenings from the balcony we looked down upon Constantine, lying at our feet in the bluish moonlight...." At last, in August Madame Maraud insisted that he should go away, return to his work; and during his journey he wrote: "I'm going away! I am going away, poisoned by the bitter sweet of parting! She gave me a remembrance, a velvet ribbon which she wore round her neck as a young girl. At the last moment she blessed me, and I saw tears shine in her eyes, when she said: 'Good-bye, my dear son.'"

Was he right in thinking that Madam Maraud was also happy in August? No one knows. But that his leaving was painful to her--there is no doubt of that. That word "son," which had often troubled her before, now had a sound for her which she could not bear to hear. Formerly when friends met her on the way to church, and said to her jokingly: "What have you to pray for, Madame Maraud? You are already without sin and without troubles!" she more than once answered with a sad smile: "I complain to God that he has not given me a son." Now the thought of a son never left her, the thought of the happiness that he would constantly give her by his mere existence in the world. And once, soon after Emile's departure, she said to her husband:

"Now I understand it all. I now believe firmly that every mother ought to have a son, that every mother who has no son, if she look into her own heart and examine her whole life, will realize that she is unhappy. You are a man and cannot feel that, but it is so....Oh how tenderly, passionately a woman can love a son!"

She was very affectionate to her husband during that autumn. It would happen sometimes that, sitting alone with him, she would suddenly say bashfully:

"Listen, Hector....I am ashamed to mention it again to you, but still ...do you ever think of March, '76? Ah, if we had had a son!"

"All this troubled me a good deal," M. Maraud said later, "and it troubled me the more because she began to get thin and out of health. She grew feeble, became more and more silent and gentle. She went out to our friends more and more rarely, she avoided going to town unless compelled....I have no doubt that some terrible, incomprehensible disease had been gradually getting hold of her, body and soul!" And the governess added that that autumn, Madame Maraud, if she went out, invariably put on a thick white veil, which she had never done before, and that, on coming home, she would immediately take it off in front of the glass and would carefully examine her tired face. It is unnecessary to explain what had been going on in her soul during that period. But did she desire to see Emile? Did he write to her and did she answer him? He produced before the court two telegrams which he alleged she sent him in reply to letters of his. One was dated November 10: "You are driving me mad. Be calm. Send me a message immediately." The other of December 23: "No, no, don't come, I implore you. Think of me, love me as a mother." But, of course, the truth that the telegrams had been sent by her could not be proved. Only this is certain, that from September to January the life which Madame Maraud lived was miserable, agitated, morbid.

The late autumn of that year in Constantine was cold and rainy. Then, as is always the case in Algeria, there suddenly came a delightful spring. And a liveliness began again to return to Madame Maraud, that happy, subtle intoxication which people who have already lived through their youth feel at the blossoming of spring. She began to go out again; she drove out a good deal with the children and used to take them to the deserted garden of the villa Hashim; she intended to go to Algiers, and to show the children Blida near which there is in the hills a wooded gorge, the favourite haunt of monkeys. And so it went on until January 17 of the year 1893. On January 17 she woke up with a feeling of gentle happiness which, it seemed, had agitated her the whole night. Her husband was away on business, and in his absence she slept alone in the large room; the blinds and curtains made it almost dark. Still from the pale bluishness which filtered in one could see that it was very early. And, indeed, the little watch on the night table showed that it was six o'clock. She felt with delight the morning freshness coming from the garden, and, wrapping the light blanket round her, turned to the wall...."Why am I so happy?" she thought as she fell asleep. And in vague and beautiful visions she saw scenes in Italy and Sicily, scenes of that far-off spring when she sailed in a cabin, with its windows opening on to the deck and the cold silvery sea, with doorhangings which time had worn and faded to a rusty silver colour, with its threshold of brass shining from perpetual polishings.... Then she saw boundless bays, lagoons, low shores, an Arab city all white with flat roofs and behind it misty blue hills and mountains. It was Tunis, where she had only once been, that spring when she was in Naples, Palermo....But then, as though the chill of a wave had passed over her, with a start, she opened her eyes. It was past eight; she heard the voices of the children and the governess. She got up, put on a wrap, and, going out on to the balcony, went down to the garden and sat in the rocking-chair. It stood on the sand by a round table under a blossoming mimosa tree which made a golden arbour heavily scented in the sun. The maid brought her coffee. She again began to think of Tunis, and she remembered the strange thing which had happened to her there, the sweet terror and happy silence of the moment before death which she had experienced in that pale-blue city in a warm pink twilight, half lying in a rocking-chair on the hotel roof, faintly seeing the dark face of the Arab hypnotizer and juggler, who squatted in front of her and sent her to sleep by his hardly audible, monotonous melodies and the slow movements of his thin hands. And suddenly, as she was thinking and was looking mechanically with wide-open eyes at the bright silver spark which shone in the sunlight from the spoon in the glass of water, she lost consciousness.... When with a start she opened her eyes again, Emile was standing over her.

All that followed after that unexpected meeting is known from the words of Emile himself, from his story, from his answers in cross-examination. "Yes, I came to Constantine out of the blue!" he said; "I came because I felt that the Powers of Heaven themselves could not stop me. In the morning of January 17 straight from the railway station, without any warning, I arrived at M. Maraud's house and ran into the garden. I was overwhelmed by what I saw, but no sooner had I taken a step forward than she woke up. She seemed to be amazed both by the unexpectedness of my appearance and by what had been happening to her, but she uttered no cry. She looked at me like a person who has just woken up from a sound sleep, and then she got up, arranging her hair.

"It is just what I anticipated," she said without expression; "you did not obey me!"

And with a characteristic movement she folded the wrap round her bosom, and taking my head in her two hands kissed me twice on the forehead.

I was bewildered with passionate ecstasy, but she quietly pushed me from her and said:

"Come, I am not dressed; I'll be back presently; go to the children."

"But, for the love of God, what was the matter with you just now?" I asked, following her on to the balcony.

"Oh, it was nothing, a slight faintness; I had been looking at the shining spoon," she answered, regaining control of herself, and beginning to speak with animation. "But what have you done, what have you done!"

I could not find the children anywhere; it was empty and quiet in the house. I sat in the dining-room, and heard her suddenly begin to sing in a distant room in a strong, melodious voice, but I did not understand then the full horror of that singing, because I was trembling with nervousness. I had not slept at all all night; I had counted the minutes while the train was hurrying me to Constantine; I jumped into the first carriage I met, raced out of the station; I did not expect as I came to the town.... I knew I, too, had a foreboding that my coming would be fatal to us; but still what I saw in the garden, that mystical meeting, and that sudden change in her attitude towards me, I could not expect that! In ten minutes she came down with her hair dressed, in a light grey dress with a shade of blue in it.

"Ah," she said, while I kissed her hand, "I forgot that to-day is Sunday; the children are at church, and I overslept.... After church the children will go to the pine-wood--have you ever been there?"

And, without waiting for my answer, she rang the bell, and told them to bring me coffee. She began to look fixedly at me, and, without listening to my replies, to ask me how I lived, and what I was doing; she began to speak of herself, of how, after two or three very bad months during which she had become "terribly old"--those words were uttered with an imperceptible smile--she now felt so well, as young, as never before.... I answered, listened, but a great deal I did not understand. Both of us said meaningless things; my hands grew cold at the thought of another terrible and inevitable hour. I do not deny that I felt as though I were struck by lightning when she said "I have grown old...." I suddenly noticed that she was right; in the thinness of her hands, and faded, though youthful, face, in the dryness of some of the outlines of her figure, I noticed the first signs of that which, painfully and somehow awkwardly--but still more painfully--makes one's heart contract at the sight of an ageing woman. Oh yes, how quickly and sharply she had changed, I thought. But still she was beautiful; I grew intoxicated looking at her. I had been accustomed to dream of her endlessly; I had never for an instant forgotten when, in the evening of July 11, I had embraced her knees for the first time. Her hands, too, trembled slightly, as she arranged her hair and spoke and smiled and looked at me; and suddenly--you will understand the whole catastrophic power of that woman--suddenly that smile somehow became distorted, and she said with difficulty, but yet firmly:

"You must go home, you must rest after your journey--you are not looking yourself; your eyes are so terribly suffering, your lips so burning that I cannot bear it any longer....Would you like me to come with you, to accompany you?"

And, without waiting for my answer, she got up and went to put on her hat and cloak....

We drove quickly to the villa Hashim. I stopped for a moment on the terrace to pick some flowers. She did not wait for me, but opened the door herself. I had no servants; there was only a watchman, but he did not see us. When I came into the hall, hot and dark with its drawn blinds, and gave her the flowers, she kissed them; then, putting one arm round me, she kissed me. Her lips were dry from excitement, but her voice was clear.

"But listen ... how shall we ... have you got anything?" she asked.

At first I did not understand her; I was so overwhelmed by the first kiss, the first endearment, and I murmured:

"What do you mean?"

She shrank back.

"What!" she said, almost sternly. "Did you imagine that I... that we can live after this? Have you anything to kill ourselves with?"

I understood, and quickly showed her my revolver, loaded with five cartridges, which I always kept on me.

She walked away quickly ahead of me from one room to the other. I followed her with that numbness of the senses with which a naked man on a sultry day walks out into the sea; I heard the rustle of her skirts. At last we were there; she threw off her cloak and began to untie the strings of her hat. Her hands were still trembling and in the half-light I again noticed something, pitiful and tired in her face....

But she died with firmness. At the last moment she was transformed; she kissed me, and moving her head back so as to see my face, she whispered to me such tender and moving words that I cannot repeat them.

I wanted to go out and pick some flowers to strew on the death-bed. She would not let me; she was in a hurry and said:

"No, no, you must not ... there are flowers here ... here are your flowers," and she kept on repeating: "And see, I beseech you by all that is sacred to you, kill me!"

"Yes, and then I will kill myself," I said, without for a moment doubting my resolution.

"Oh, I believe you, I believe you," she answered, already apparently half-unconscious....

A moment before her death she said very quietly and simply:

"My God, this is unspeakable!"

And again:

"Where are the flowers you gave me? Kiss me--for the last time."

She herself put the revolver to her head. I wanted to do it, but she stopped me:

"No, that is not right; let me do it. Like this, my child....And *afterwards* make the sign of the cross over me and lay the flowers on my heart...."

When I fired, she made a slight movement with her lips, and I fired again....

She lay quiet; in her dead face there was a kind of bitter happiness. Her hair was loose; the tortoise-shell comb lay on the floor. I staggered to my feet in order to put an end to myself. But the room, despite the blinds, was light; in the light and stillness which suddenly surrounded me, I saw clearly her face already pale....And suddenly madness seized me; I rushed to the window, undid and threw open the shutters, began shouting and firing into the air.... The rest you know...."

[In the spring, five years ago, while wandering in Algeria, the writer of these lines visited Constantine....There often comes to him a memory of the cold, rainy, and yet spring evenings which he spent by the fire in the reading-room of a certain old and homely French hotel. In the heavy, elaborate book-case were much-read illustrated papers, and in them you could see the faded photographs of Madame Maraud. There were photographs taken of her at different ages, and among them the Lausanne portrait of her as a girl....Her story is told here once more, from a desire to tell it in one's own way.]

THE HOGARTH PRESS
PARADISE ROAD, RICHMOND, SURREY

PREVIOUS PUBLICATIONS
CLIVE BELL
Poems.
2*s*.6*d*.net.
T. S. ELIOT
Poems.
Out of print.
E. M. FORSTER
The Story of the Siren.
2*s*.6*d*.net.
ROGER FRY
Twelve Original Woodcuts. Third impression.
5*s*.net.
MAXIM GORKY
Reminiscences of Tolstoi. Second edition.
5*s*.net.
KATHERINE MANSFIELD
Prelude.
3*s*.6*d*.net.
HOPE MIRRLEES
Paris. A Poem.
Out of print.
J. MIDDLETON MURRY
The Critic in Judgment.
2*s*.6*d*.net.
LOGAN PEARSALL SMITH
Stories from the Old Testament retold.
4*s*.6*d*.net.
The Note-books of ANTON TCHEKHOV, together with
Reminiscences of TCHEKHOV by Maxim Gorky.
5*s*.net.
LEONARD WOOLF
Stories of the East.
3*s*.net.
VIRGINIA WOOLF
Monday or Tuesday.

4*s*.6*d*.net.
The Mark on the Wall. Second edition.
1*s*.6*d*.net.
Kew Gardens.
Out of print.
LEONARD & VIRGINIA WOOLF
Two Stories.
Out of print.

Forthcoming Publications
KARN. A Poem. By Ruth Manning-Sanders.
3*s*. 6*d*. net.
DAYBREAK. A Book of Poems. By Fredegond

Shove. 3*s*. 6*d*. net.
THE GENTLEMAN FROM SAN FRANCISCO

and other Stories. By I. A. Bunin. Translated
from the Russian by S. S. Koteliansky and
Leonard Woolf.

www.ingramcontent.com/pod-product-compliance
Lightning Source LLC
LaVergne TN
LVHW021711210726
843510LV00015B/1406